# STITCHING STARS

# STITCHING STARS

## THE STORY QUILTS OF HARRIET POWERS

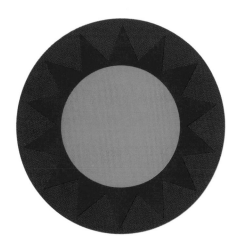

## MARY E. LYONS

CHARLES SCRIBNER'S SONS · NEW YORK
Maxwell Macmillan Canada · Toronto
Maxwell Macmillan International
New York · Oxford · Singapore · Sydney

### ACKNOWLEDGMENTS

I am grateful to the National Endowment for the Humanities and the DeWitt Wallace Reader's Digest Fund for the Teacher-Scholar Award that provided the time and financial support necessary to research the life of Harriet Powers.

Thanks to Helen Istvan, who helped me begin, and to Shantron Michie, who helped me finish. Special thanks to music educator Wayne Burgess, folklorist Dr. Charles Perdue of the University of Virginia, and Bill Gilcher of the University of Maryland Visual Press.

Charles Scribner's Sons Books for Young Readers
Macmillan Publishing Company
866 Third Avenue, New York, NY 10022

Maxwell Macmillan Canada, Inc.
1200 Eglinton Avenue East, Suite 200
Don Mills, Ontario M3C 3N1

Macmillan Publishing Company is part of the Maxwell Communication Group of Companies.

**First edition**    10  9  8  7  6  5  4  3  2  1
**Printed in Hong Kong**
**Book design by Vikki Sheatsley**

Library of Congress Cataloging-in-Publication Data
Lyons, Mary (Mary E.)
  Stitching stars : the story quilts of Harriet Powers / Mary E. Lyons. — 1st ed.      p.      cm.
  Includes bibliographical references and index.
  Summary: An illustrated biography of the African American quilter who made quilts of her favorite Bible stories and folk tales.
  ISBN 0-684-19576-3
1. Patchwork—Juvenile literature.    2. Afro-American quilts—Georgia—History—Juvenile literature.    3. Powers, Harriet, 1837–1911—Juvenile literature.    4. Afro-American quiltmakers—Georgia—Biography—Juvenile literature. [1. Powers, Harriet, 1837–1911. 2. Quiltmakers. 3. Afro-Americans—Biography. 4. Quilts. 5. Patchwork.]    I. Title.
TT835.L95  1993      746.9'7'092—dc20      [B]  92-38561

*To Nonny Hogrogrian Kherdian*

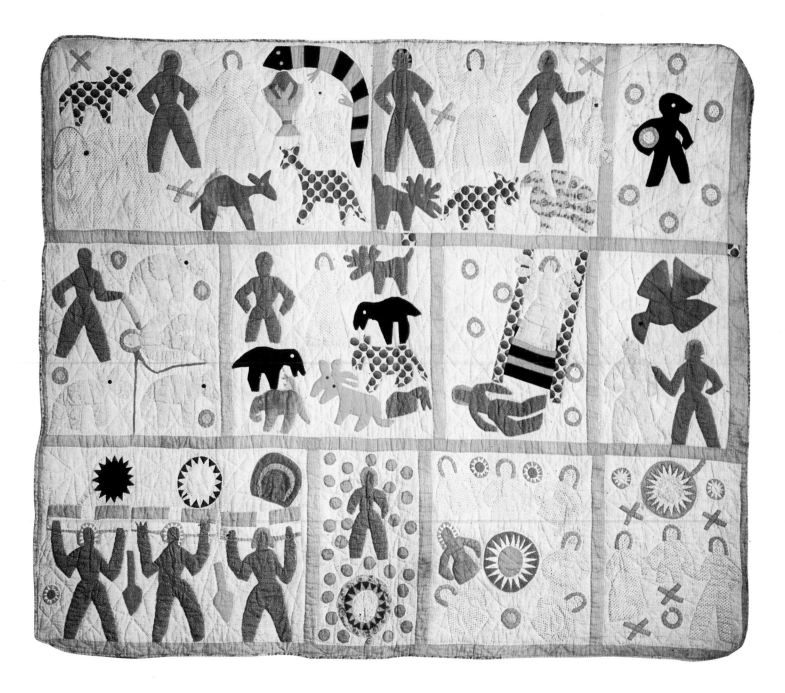

Harriet Powers was the mother of eleven children: nine boys and girls and a pair of story quilts. One by one, most of her babies grew up and left home, as children usually do. Harriet felt a little lonely when they moved out. The little Georgia farmhouse seemed too quiet and empty. Sometime around 1886 she decided to start another child: a story quilt.

She had sewn many other quilts in her forty-nine years. Each was made from scraps of old clothes and held together with thousands of stitches. Each had been a loyal companion, always there to cover her chilled bones. But the new quilt would be more than just a coverlet. It would be a diary of her spiritual life.

Harriet was a person of deep religious feelings. She had grown up hearing Bible stories about the Garden of Eden, the Baptism of Christ, and the Last Supper. The people in the Bible—Adam and Eve, Cain and Abel, Jacob and Judas—were so familiar that they seemed to be part of her family. Making a quilt of their stories would be like putting down her own history. Instead of using pen, ink, and paper, she would write with needle, thread, and cloth.

Harriet's first story-quilt. Broken vertical strips divide the pictures. Similar designs can be found in woven cloth from West Africa, where some believe that "evil travels in straight lines." Crooked lines will startle any spirits that may be lurking about. Such surprises are common in African-American culture: The congregation calls out, "Amen!" to agree with the minister's sermon; the guitar player suddenly plays a "hot lick"; a dancer quickly "breaks" to the ground, then returns to an upright position.

*"Slavery time when I was chillun down on marster's plantation."*

GEORGIA BAKER

Harriet Powers was born into slavery on October 29, 1837. Nothing is known about the first eighteen years of her life. Like the pink and green colors in her first story quilt, details of her younger years have faded with time. But the words of former Georgia slaves let us imagine a picture of her youth. If we listen to their voices, we can hear her speak.

Census records show that Harriet lived over half of her life in Clarke County, Georgia. It is likely that she was born there or in a nearby county. This section of the state has been called the Plantation Belt. A plantation was a farm with more than twenty slaves, and there were many such farms in the area.

Harriet Powers was probably born and raised a plantation slave. When she was three years old, there were seventy-one plantations in Clarke County alone. It was these planters who held more than half of Clarke County's five thousand African Americans in slavery. The rest of the slaves lived on small farms or in Athens, the only town in Clarke County.

We can be certain that Harriet learned how to sew when she was a young girl. Slave women were always involved in the making of textiles, whether on a plantation or a smaller farm. Harriet grew up watching older women card cotton, spin thread, weave and dye cloth, and sew clothes and bedding. "Grandma lived in the same house with Ma and us chillun," remembered a former slave, "and she worked in the loom house and wove cloth all the time. She wove the checkidy cloth for the slaves' clothes and she made flannel cloth, too."

Since many black women were expert needleworkers, Harriet surely learned to sew from her own mother. One daughter of a former slave proudly remembered her mother as "a fine seamstress." The planter's wife also might have been her sewing teacher. "Young girls must be taught to sew," wrote the mistress of Hull plantation in Clarke County, "and the plantation hands must be provided with clothes."

Often the wife did not sew herself but su-

Many African-American women spun thread at night on a spinning wheel such as this one. *Alderman Library, Special Collections, University of Virginia.*

pervised the labor. The mistress of Hull remembered that "after breakfast, work was cut out for the sempstresses." And an ex-slave recollected that her mistress, Miss Julia, "bossed" the whole cutting and sewing operation.

Some plantation owners provided a yearly change of clothing for the slaves. But these soon wore out. The daughter of a slave on a Clarke County plantation recalled that her mother sewed all day for the slaveholder's family. Only at night could she make addi-

tional clothes for her own family. Fabric was scarce, so slave children like Harriet usually owned only one set of clothing at a time. In the summer she wore a homespun cotton dress over a pair of underwear called "drawers." In the winter she wore a "sack." This shapeless overcoat was made of "heavy yarn," or cloth woven with one strand of wool and one strand of cotton.

Sewing didn't end with the making of clothes. Some former slaves remembered that the master gave them one blanket a year,

As a child, Harriet would have worn a dress like this one. *Alderman Library, Special Collections, University of Virginia.*

often at Christmas. But one blanket could not keep a body warm on a frosty January night. Most slave women had to make extra coverlets and quilts.

Quilts were as common as corn bread. And they were just as essential for survival. As a little girl Harriet slept on a "Georgia" bed made of hard planks. Thick ropes served as springs. The mattress was stuffed with scratchy straw called "Georgy" feathers. At least these uncomfortable cotlike beds had "plenty of quilts and cover," according to one ex-slave. Quilts softened Harriet's rough bunk. They also kept her from freezing in the winter.

Harriet washed her quilts and clothes by hand. Imagine taking a bath like the one she would have given a quilt. First, she filled an iron pot with water from the well. Then she poured strong lye soap from a jug into the water and lit a fire under the pot. When the water boiled, she added the quilt and stirred. After the suds foamed, she removed the quilt and beat it on a block with sticks to "fetch the dirt out." One Georgia slave remembered, "On wash days you could hear them battling sticks pounding every which-a-way." As a little girl Harriet would have

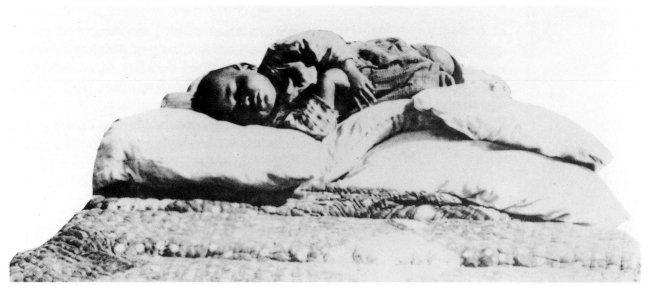
Quilts helped Harriet sleep as soundly as this little girl. *The Library of Congress.*

waited for the water to cool, then climbed right into the pot with bare feet and stomped the dirt out of the poor quilt.

Quilts had to be sturdy to endure years of hard use. Because they were so well made, they were as valuable as money. Some slaveholders allowed black women to sell their quilts for cash. Quilts were often given as prizes at buck-dancing contests held by the slaves. When Northern soldiers raided Southern farms during the Civil War, they stole horses, gold, and quilts.

Quilts were precious items. But they also provided beauty, fun, and even romance to ease the hard times of slavery. Saturday nights in winter were long and lonely. January was too late for corn-shucking parties and too soon for pea-shelling frolics. So the women in Harriet's quarters went from one plantation to another for quilting bees. Everybody knew that a "parcel" of women could quilt better than one.

Down came the wooden quilting frame that hung by four ropes from the cabin raf-

Washday. *Alderman Library, Special Collections, University of Virginia.*

ters. Then a great scraping of wood on wood commenced as the women shoved their oak-split chairs across the floor and up to the frame. Young girls like Harriet were allowed to help their mothers stitch and sing, gossip and giggle. Sometimes they even crawled under the quilt and lay flat on their backs— a perfect spot to watch quick hands work the needles up and down, down and up.

This was one of the rare moments when the women had time to themselves. The mistress supervised their cutting and stitching during the day. But a quilting bee was private. Each woman could be an artist with scissors and cloth. Even the menfolk were not allowed in until the quilting was over. For a few hours, needlework set the enslaved women free.

Usually they made plain quilts from large squares of fabric in a single color or print. Other quilts were fancy, with scraps of fabric pieced into intricate patterns. Sometimes the women used the mistress's patterns, designs with names like Flying Geese and Rising Sun. Just as often they made up their own designs by piecing together long strips of cloth. Every quilt was beautiful in its own way. An ex-slave said when she showed off her sunburst quilt, "Hit's poetry, ain't it?"

Some quilting parties were run as competitions. An appointed quilting "manager" was the coach. "At quilting bees," recollected a former slave, "four folks was put at every quilt, one at every corner. These quilts had been pieced up by old slaves who warn't able to work in the field. . . . A prize was always give to the four which finished their quilt first. Refreshments went along with

A scene from Harriet Powers's first story-quilt. Adam and Eve are naming animals in the Garden of Eden: three camels, an elephant, an ostrich, a sea monster, and a serpent.

Adam and Eve are still in Paradise. Eve has "conceived and bared a son." He is wearing pantaloons and petting a chicken. The bird of Paradise is in the lower right corner. The bird's original green and red colors have faded to pink and brown.

this, too." Two or three quilts might be made in one night. Only when the sewing was done could the men come in for a "quilting feast" of pies, cakes, chicken, and brandied peaches.

Dancing followed the food. The inventive slaves had a knack for making something out of nothing, including their music. "Stretch cow-hides over cheese-boxes and you had tambourines," said an ex-slave from Harriet's county. "Saw bones from a cow, knock them together and call it a drum. Or use broom-straw on fiddle-strings and you had your entire band."

Young folks like Harriet went to quiltings to flirt as much as to sew. According to one former slave, both the men and women were "glad to get together." Harriet may have met her future husband, Armstead Powers, at a quilting frolic. They danced the Buzzard Lope, sang "You steal my true love, and I steal your'en," and fell in love along the way.

When Harriet and Armstead decided to marry, they had to get permission from the slaveholder. The young couple were married in a broomstick wedding. Everybody in the quarters went to the ceremony. First, a straw broom as big around as an arm and five feet long was placed on the ground. Then family and friends gathered in a circle for the service.

An ex-slave recalled the words: "The preacher would say to the man, 'Do you take this woman to be you wife?' He says, 'Yes.' 'Well, jump the broom.' After he jumped, the preacher would say the same to the woman. When she jumped the preacher said, 'I pronounce you man and wife.' " A dance and supper usually followed the wedding.

If Harriet and Armstead were owned by the same slaveholder, they lived together in the same cabin. If not, Armstead had to carry a piece of paper signed by the master to leave his plantation. With this pass he could visit Harriet twice a week, on Wednesday and Saturday nights.

## • 1855–1865 •

"What does I remember about the war? Well, it was fit to fetch our freedom."

*CALLIE ELDER*

Harriet was eighteen and Armstead was twenty-two when their daughter Amanda was born in 1855. They may have had more children by the start of the Civil War in 1861—the bloodiest conflict the United States has ever known. The war was fought to end slavery. But sadly, the slaves suffered along with everyone else. These were frightful times for the Powers family.

More than 50 percent of the men in Clarke County were wounded, killed, or died of disease over the next four years. Many of them were black, since healthy male slaves were "volunteered" by their masters for service with the Confederate army. There were severe shortages of food, medicine, and clothing for those who stayed behind.

Women remade and patched old clothes until they turned to rags. Cloth, thread, even buttons were scarce. When Harriet mended her family's dresses and shirts, she used per-

Harriet's playful-looking Satan is like the devil in African-American folktales. He is a trickster and conjure man, not an evil spirit. When Harriet identified this picture as "Satan amidst the seven stars," she repeated the *S* sound five times. Poets often use the same trick to catch the reader's attention. Slaves, too, repeated letter sounds when making up religious songs:

Wrestle with Satan and wrestle with sin,
Stepped over hell and come back again.

simmon seeds instead of shell buttons. By the end of the war, some people in her county paid for food with rare factory-made thread instead of worthless Confederate money.

The Powers family lived in fear of the bloodshed of war. But the town of Athens was spared the fighting that wrecked much of the South. The Union army did not enter the town until after surrender. Meanwhile, some slaves secretly hoped that they would come. One ex-slave remembered going to church in Athens with her mistress. When the white preacher prayed that the Northerners would be turned back, she silently begged, "Oh, Lord, please send the Yankees on and let them set us free."

Athens did see violence in 1862 when a white mob hung a black man from a pine tree. In September of that same year, the Emancipation Proclamation declared that the slaves would be freed on New Year's Day, 1863. No wonder that many of the younger black men and women immediately escaped the plantations and farms where they had been held captive. Some followed the Union army. Others ran away to larger towns in Georgia or to the Northern states. If Armstead left, we know that he returned to his

Harriet said of the panel on the left, "Cain is killing his brother Abel." The dribble of red is "the stream of blood which flew over the earth." The shepherd, Abel, and his sheep are made from the same cloth. Sheep were also important animals in slave spirituals because they signified great wisdom:

Oh, the old sheep done know the road,
The young lambs must find the way.

Here Cain has gone to the land of Nod to get a wife. Harriet filled this picture with two bears, an elephant, a lion, a "kangaroo hog," a leopard with polka-dot spots, and an elk. The charming lion has one ferocious tooth. The slaves had such great respect for the lion that they often included him in their folktales and hymns. He reminded them of the courage required to run away from the slaveholder, as in this verse from "Run to Jesus, Shun the Danger":

Oh, I thought I heard them say,
There were lions in the way.

family before the end of the war. A son, Alonzo, was born in May of 1865, and another daughter, Nancy, arrived in 1866.

News of the Confederate surrender reached Athens in April of 1865. The black citizens of Clarke County were overjoyed. They built a liberty pole in the middle of town and sang and danced around it. But the celebration of freedom was short-lived.

In Athens, the aftermath of war was worse than war itself. That summer, hogs and cows ran loose in the streets. Trash piled up behind the houses. And smallpox ravaged the black population. "Them Yankees brought the smallpox here with them and give it to all the Athens folks," recalled a former slave, "and that was something awful. Folks just died out with it so bad." The epidemic doubtless killed many of Harriet's kinfolk and friends, perhaps even some of her children.

Everyone, white and black, was cheered up when the circus came to Athens at the end of 1865. Circuses had traveled through Clarke County as early as the 1820s. But this one was especially welcome, for the people had just struggled with four years of war, hunger, and death.

For seventy-five cents a ticket holder could see rhinoceroses, elephants, lions, tigers, leopards, cougars, panthers, bears, wolves, monkeys, pelicans, and macaws. Harriet probably did not go to the circus, since she thought the dancing acts were sinful. But she must have seen the circus animals parade through town at least once, for the same elephants, leopards, lions, bears, and exotic birds roam over her story quilts.

· 1866–1886 ·

"After the war I stayed on with Marse Fred and worked for wages for six years."

TOM SINGLETON

Great poverty swept through Georgia after the war. Like most people, the Powers family probably did not have enough to eat. More food had to be grown, but who would do the work? White planters were reluctant to pay for labor that so recently had been free. African Americans didn't like working for low wages in the planters' fields because that felt too much like slavery.

Competition for food was fierce. In 1866

laws were passed that forbade black people to hunt on Sunday (their only day off from work) with guns or dogs. Armstead couldn't collect fruit, berries, or honey from anyone else's land. Even fishing in local streams was restricted.

There were rumors that the federal government was giving forty-acre lots of land to the freedmen. Like other black Georgians, Harriet and Armstead longed for "forty acres and a mule" of their own. They felt ties to the earth that generations of slaves before them had cleared, tilled, plowed, and planted. When the rumors proved false, former slaves all over the South were angry and disappointed.

Some ex-slaves were able to purchase a few acres from the plantation owners. They spent money that they had put aside before the war to buy themselves out of slavery. But most had to work as field hands for eight to twelve dollars a month. They were saving for the day when they could truly be free of the white landowner.

In 1870 Armstead Powers told the census taker that he was a "farmhand." Harriet's husband probably worked for a white farmer on an all-black crew, as Georgia landowners usually hired hands of the same color. Harriet stated that her occupation was "keeping house."

But she may also have been a seamstress, the only skilled job for black women at the time. She could have earned extra money by sewing. Perhaps she made quilts or clothes to barter for other goods. Together the couple managed to collect three hundred dollars' worth (or several thousand in today's money) of personal property by 1870.

Their family continued to grow. Lizzie was born in 1868 and Marshall came along in 1872. But they still had no land of their own.

Sometime in the 1880s Harriet and Armstead became the proud owners of four acres near Sandy Creek, a black settlement north of Athens. Nine thousand years earlier, prehistoric farmers had worked this same gray dirt with axes and other tools. Cherokee Indians later settled in the area. Then white planters claimed it as their land. Now the Powers family would take a turn.

Things went well at first. Armstead was able to buy more and more farming tools. They also added horses, mules, cattle, and oxen to their stock of farm animals. The price of sewing machines had dropped by 50 per-

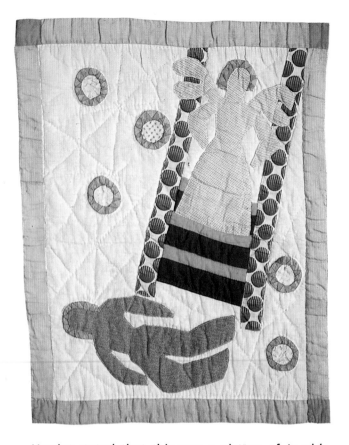

Harriet stated that this was a picture of Jacob's dream when "he lay on the ground." The slaves identified with the Bible story about Jacob, for he was homeless, hunted, and weary of his journey. The angel in Harriet's quilt is going up the ladder to heaven. In the spiritual "We Are Climbing Jacob's Ladder," the ladder also means an escape from slavery.

cent in 1878. Harriet may have bought one to use as a sewing tool.

A man's dress shirt with collar, sleeves, and wristbands required 20,530 stitches. It would have taken her days to hand-sew just one shirt. But with a machine, she could make clothes to sell at a much faster rate. She could also machine-stitch the straight seams required for a quilt.

Food was more plentiful now. The Powerses ate flathead catfish from Sandy Creek and grew their own vegetables. And they probably raised cotton.

Many small farmers in Georgia turned to cotton after the Civil War. It was an easy crop to grow, especially when commercial fertilizers became available. It was also a risky crop that was easily ruined by bad weather. But like the white planters who raised cotton before the Civil War, Armstead would have been tempted by the quick profit.

As industrialization marched through the South, life in Clarke County began to change. A waterworks brought water to Athens homes in 1882. The telephone came that same year. And in the 1890s Harriet would see electricity light up Athens houses, businesses, and streets.

With water and electric power to run the looms, cotton mills popped up all over the state, including in Clarke County. The mills bought cotton from farmers like Armstead. Then the mill workers used machines to weave cotton cloth that was shipped out on the Athens branch line railroad. Because cotton meant money, it was celebrated throughout the South. Athens held its own party with a cotton fair in 1886.

By this time Harriet had finished her first story quilt. She had cut out 299 separate pieces of cloth. Then she'd machine-stitched them to a background fabric the color of juicy pink watermelon. She'd framed each scene with bright green strips of cloth, like pictures on a wall. Finally, she'd quilted the top and bottom together with stitches that formed the outline of stars.

Here were Harriet's favorite Bible stories from spirituals she had sung all her life. And here were the Old Testament tales that she had heard the "chairbacker," or slave preacher, tell from memory at secret midnight "brush" meetings held in the woods; and the New Testament accounts that she had heard the white minister read in the plantation "praise" house before the war.

This is the Baptism of Christ. Harriet said that the bird represents "the Holy Spirit extending in the likeness of a dove." Doves appear three times in Harriet's quilts. The dove was also the most frequent bird in slave spirituals because it could easily fly away to freedom:

Sing a ho that I had the wings of a dove,
I'd fly away and be at rest.

Harriet said that the picture above "has reference to the Crucifixion." She said that the round figures were the darkness that spread over the earth. The red calico is a moon turning to blood. The slave spiritual "In That Great Getting Up Morning" also has verses about "the moon a-bleeding" and "stars a-falling." These images from the Book of Revelation were important to the slaves. They reminded them that only the moon and stars could guide a runaway slave on a dark night.

The section on the right shows Judas Iscariot, who betrayed Christ for thirty pieces of silver. The large circle is "the star that appeared in 1886 for the first time in three hundred years," an event that Harriet may have actually seen. Spirituals contained a similar mix of Bible stories and everyday events. In a religious song about a journey to Jerusalem, the slave included a line about men who patrolled the roads looking for runaways:

Patrol around me,
Thank God he no catch me.

Harriet must have felt a flush of satisfaction when she spread the quilt over her lap, traced the figures with her fingers, and studied the bright colors that bounced off each other. When she heard about the Cotton Fair, she made a decision. She would enter her quilt in the craft exhibit and introduce her new child to the rest of the world.

## • 1886–1895 •

"We didn't have no songbooks, nor couldn't read if we had 'em. We sorter made 'em up, as us went 'long."

*STEVE WEATHERSBY*

Harriet and Armstead Powers climbed into the ox cart and followed the rolling red-clay road to town. It was a glorious day for a fair. The sky was so clear that Harriet could see the hazy Blue Ridge Mountains, forty miles away.

But she was more interested in watching the child whom she held in her lap. The quilt was wrapped carefully in a sack. Harriet was anxious to get under way so that she could show it off. And she looked forward to the fair itself. This was no ordinary gathering. For the rural residents of Clarke County, the Cotton Fair was a major event.

Harriet was eager to see people dressed up in fancy clothes for the mock Cotton Wedding. And it would be a thrill to hear the gunshots and whoops of the cowboys and Indians in the Wild West show. But best of all, she might catch a glimpse of what she called the "Bible animules" before they went into the circus arena.

She hung her quilt in a corner of the exhibit tent. The aisles were lined with tables of seed displays and racks of jars with pickles and preserves. Mounds of plump potatoes, towering cotton stalks, and swollen watermelons surrounded her creation. All were competing for Best in Show.

Then a visitor strolled through the exhibit. She stopped in front of Harriet's quilt. Harriet had never seen the young woman before, but the meeting with Oneita Virginia Smith would change the fate of Harriet's story quilt forever.

Jennie Smith later remembered Harriet as being a "burnt ginger cake color." She was "an interesting woman," recalled Jennie,

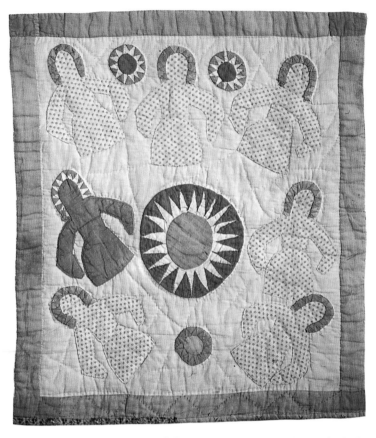

This is the story of the Last Supper. Harriet included only seven of the twelve apostles. Judas in his dark clothes stands out from all the rest.

"who loves to talk about her ole Miss and her life before the war." But Jennie was an art teacher at a local girls' school, and it was Harriet's quilt that fascinated her the most. "I regret exceedingly," she later wrote about the quilt, "that it is impossible to describe the gorgeous coloring of the work."

Jennie Smith knew the quilt was a rare work of art. She immediately offered to buy it. Harriet was shocked. How could she give up her beloved stories? The quilt was not for sale at any price!

But four years later Harriet and Armstead needed money. Clarke County had more small farmers than any other part of the state. So many farmers had cotton to sell that the price dropped to five cents a pound. Harriet remembered the woman who had wanted to buy her quilt. She sent word to Jennie Smith that it was for sale.

Typical wages for a black craftsperson in Georgia in 1890 were as low as $1 a day. Black labor was so cheap that Harriet may not have thought her quilt was worth much. She probably asked little for it, but Jennie Smith later recalled, "My financial affairs were at a low ebb and I could not purchase."

Another year passed. The Powerses were

desperate. Sometime in 1891 Armstead sold two acres of land for $177. When Jennie sent a message that she could now buy the quilt, Harriet wrapped it in a clean flour sack as tenderly as she would a baby. Then she put the whole bundle in a large burlap crocus sack to keep it safe from harm. The Powerses climbed in the ox cart and made the slow trip to Athens.

Harriet arrived at Jennie's house at 129 Washington Street holding the cherished cargo on her lap. She asked ten dollars for the quilt. But the art teacher said that she "only had five to give." Harriet trudged back to the cart for a talk with her husband. She returned to Jennie Smith's porch. "Owin to de hardness of de times," she said with deep regret, "my old man allows I'd better take hit."

She felt a little better when Jennie told her she could visit her "child" at any time. And she almost smiled when Jennie promised to save all her scraps so Harriet could make another. But her face turned as solemn as a sermon when she explained each story in the quilt. "We can't go back any further than the Bible," she told Jennie.

The art teacher wrote down some of her

Oneita Virginia (Jennie) Smith as a young woman. *Alderman Library, Special Collections, University of Virginia.*

Harriet told Jennie Smith, "The next history is the Holy Family: Joseph, the Virgin, and the infant Jesus with the star of Bethlehem over his head. Those are the crosses he had to bear through his undergoing. Anything for wisement. We can't go back any further than the Bible."

exact words. They reveal that sewing the story quilt was a religious act for Harriet, like singing a spiritual. African Americans could choose any story in the Bible and make up a song about it. In the same way, Harriet could pick a favorite story from the Old or New Testament and create a picture for it.

And just as the slaves had sung moving melodies without songbooks, Harriet needed no pattern book to make the delightful figures in her quilt. She cut each shape to suit her. Then she "eyeballed" its placement on the cloth. With the vision of a true artist, she worked from the pictures in her head and the music in her heart.

Even the squares in the quilt resemble a typical black spiritual. They produce their own "swingy" rhythm. In the outline of Harriet's quilt (figure B, page 21), imagine each square as a beat. Clap your hands once for every square. Some of the squares, or beats, are longer than others. They receive a longer clap that slows down the rhythm. But when you clap quickly for the shorter "beats," the rhythm catches up. This is called syncopation, and it is a common feature of African-American music.

The words and notes in the quilt outline

## JOHN, JOHN

FIGURE A

come from a spiritual sung by Georgia slaves called *John, John* (figure A). Harriet may or may not have sung this particular song. But its African-American pulse beats in her story quilt: The first three measures of the chorus roughly match the three rows of the quilt outline in figure B. To complete the first sentence in the chorus, add the word *John* at the end of the third row.

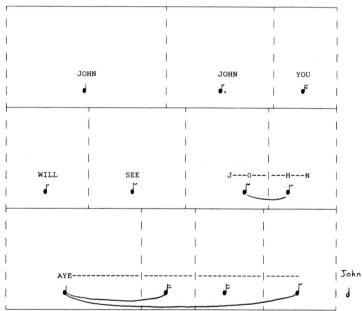

FIGURE B

## • 1895–1898 •

*"I went to heaven in de spirit and see with the eye of faith. An angel take me and show me de stars, how they hang there by a silver chord, and de moon just a ball of blood."*

OPHELIA JEMISON

For Harriet, giving up the quilt was as hard as selling half of her and Armstead's land. But it meant that her glorious needlework would never be forgotten. "It is my intention," Jennie wrote in 1891, "to exhibit this quilt in the Colored Building at the Cotton States Exposition in Atlanta. . . ."

The international exposition opened in September of 1895. It was a world's fair—a crowning ceremony for the royal crop of cotton. The exposition also gave countries an occasion to show off their new inventions and machines. Participating nations included the United States, Brazil, Argentina, England, France, Germany, Russia, and Italy. Jennie knew this was an unusual chance to share Harriet's genius with art lovers from around the world.

The city officials of Atlanta built a rolling grassy park and a lake especially for the event. Mammoth exhibition halls were constructed. Visitors to the exposition thought they had been suddenly transported to a foreign land: the kingdom of Cotton. The administration building looked like a medieval fortress, complete with towers. Colorful flags perched on top of the castle turrets and rippled through the autumn air.

The "Negro" Building that held Harriet's quilt was almost as big as a football field. Visitors looking for needlework walked through the main entrance and turned left. They passed tables of delicious breads and biscuits, crackers and cakes, all made by African-American bakers from every state.

The needlework exhibit was the largest in the building. There were 123 items on display: lace of gold and silver thread, fancy pins and needles, tapestries, even wigs. Jennie Smith may have entered Harriet's quilt too late to be listed in the catalog, but we know that faculty wives from Atlanta University saw it. They arranged to have Harriet make a quilt for the Reverend Charles Hall, chairman of the board of trustees of Atlanta University.

The second quilt would be a little different from the first. Once again Harriet would re-

The "Negro" Building at the Cotton States Exposition was built entirely by black craftspeople with $10,000 raised by the black community. *Alderman Library, Special Collections, University of Virginia.*

tell tales that she had heard all her life. But for this quilt she decided to mix religious stories with folktales about the weather. Weather was important to rural Georgians. It affected their crops and their income. African-American farmers, especially, told stories about the weather because they had no other way to record it.

As slaves they had been forbidden to read and write. In 1850 few of the slaves in Clarke County could read a word or sign their names. The first public school in the county for African Americans didn't open until 1886, so many were still illiterate, like Harriet. If they wanted to remember something important, they turned it into a story. Then

Harriet's second story-quilt. Here the figures seem to be in constant motion. They wave, walk, kneel, put hands on hips, and blow the trumpet. Stripes, polka dots, and other patterns also add movement to her pictures. The contrast of light and dark colors fills the quilt with life and power.

they told the story to family and friends.

Harriet's way of retelling stories was sewing. She remembered weather incidents so well that "reading" her second quilt is like reading a book about the weather. Two of the weather stories in her quilt happened before she was born: the Dark Day of 1780 and the Falling of the Stars in 1833. Both pictures recall the real events.

On May 19, 1780, the skies of New England turned dark as night. Sooty, greasy rain fell. It thickened the rivers and filled the air with ashes. One witness wrote in his diary that he had to eat lunch by candlelight. Another described the "fowls fleeing, bewildered, to their roosts, and the cattle returning to their stalls."

No one realized that distant forest fires burning in Canada had caused the darkness. Many people thought that the end of the world had come. Ministers warned that the Dark Day was a warning from God. They quoted chapter six, verse twelve from Revelation: "The sun became black as sackcloth of hair." Both the Bible verse and the Dark Day, they said, were proof that God's judgment and the end of the world were at hand.

Over a hundred years later, Harriet

In Harriet's words: "Job praying for his enemies. Job's crosses. Job's coffin." Like Job in the Bible, Harriet was tested by hard times, bad luck, and poverty.

"The dark day of May 19, 1780. The seven stars were seen 12.N. in the day. The cattle all went to bed, chickens to roost, and the trumpet was blown. The sun went off to a small spot and then to darkness."

learned about the Dark Day, probably from a preacher. How did the Dark Day story travel from New England to Georgia? Why did Harriet hear about it in church? African-American ministers were like storytellers. Just as Bruh Rabbit folktales were told and retold in black communities, preachers passed pieces of sermons to each other down through the generations.

Like African griots who could recite the entire history of their people, the preachers served as keepers of the past. Those who couldn't read developed amazing memories. They could recall a vast number of Bible verses, hymns, and spectacular stories like the one about the Dark Day. These became the ingredients of sermons that sang with poetry, drama, and a syncopated musical rhythm. "I see the sun when she turned herself black," chanted a black preacher in Augusta, Georgia, in 1867. "I see the stars a fallin from the sky. . . ."

On the night of November 13, 1833, showers of shooting stars did seem to set the sky ablaze. Every hour, eight to ten thousand meteors shot through space like soundless fireworks. Some left strands of yellow, bloodred, or greenish blue light that glowed for fifteen minutes. Others looked as big as the moon. The flash was so bright that it woke up sleeping Georgians. One man described it as "one of the most splendid sights perhaps that mortal eyes have ever beheld."

Harriet was born just four years after this major meteorological event. She grew up hearing folks speak with wonder in their voices about the night the stars fell like snow.

After November 13, 1833, scientists began to study meteors. Now they know that a billion meteors enter the earth's atmosphere every day. Most break apart completely before reaching the earth. But people in Harriet's time thought that meteor showers, like the Dark Day, were connected somehow to stories in the Bible.

Harriet recorded their beliefs: "The people were frighten," she said of the meteor storm in 1833, "and thought that the end of time had come." But from her words, we know that she also thought God was merciful: "God's hand staid the stars."

She actually experienced two of the four weather stories that were stitched into the quilt: the Red Light Night of 1846 and the Cold Thursday of February 1895. Again, the names that she gave to both pictures

The falling of stars on November 13, 1833. "The people were frighten and thought that the end of time had come. God's hand staid the stars. The varmints rushed out of their beds."

"Cold Thursday, 10 of Feb. 1895. A woman frozen while at prayer. A woman frozen at a gateway. A man with a sack of meal frozen. Isicles formed from the breath of a mule. All blue birds killed. A man frozen at his jug of liquor."

"The red light night of 1846. A man tolling the bell to notify the people of the wonder. Women, children, and fowls frightened but God's merciful hand caused no harm to them."

match the weather conditions for those dates.

The glowing meteor showers of the Red Light Night in 1846 were visible in the southeastern United States. It's likely that Harriet could see them in the skies of upper Georgia. And on February 8 through February 10, 1895, Athens had rare snow and subzero temperatures. Harriet recorded four deaths in her picture of this cold snap. It was certainly cold enough to kill anyone exposed to the frigid temperatures, especially people in the Deep South, who only had clothes for mild winter conditions.

Harriet may have heard the story of the "rich people who were taught nothing of God" in Sunday school. In this scene she placed a clock between Bob Johnson and Kate Bell to show that they had gone to their "everlasting punishment." In both European and African-American folklore, clocks were related to bad luck and death. As signified in Harriet's picture, black Georgians often placed a clock on a grave to wake the dead on Judgment Day.

Free-traveling pigs ("as independent as a hog on ice" and "road hog") are common in folklore, and one appears in Harriet's second quilt. Her story about Betts, the independent

"Rich people who were taught nothing of God. Bob Johnson and Kate Bell of Virginia. They told their parents to stop the clock at one and tomorrow it would strike one and so it did. This was the signal that they had entered everlasting punishment. The independent hog which ran 500 miles from Ga. to Va. her name was Betts."

"John baptizing Christ and the spirit of God descending and rested upon his shoulder like a dove."

"The serpent lifted up by Mosses and women bringing their children to look upon it to be healed." Moses was a popular hero in the slaves' religious songs, for he led his people out of captivity to freedom:

Go down, Moses,
Way down in Egypt land.
Tell ol' Pharaoh,
Let my people go.

pig, may have been a combination of folklore and local legend. If it really happened, the facts are buried in the Long Ago. Still, her mileage is amazingly correct: The distance from Athens, Georgia, to Richmond, Virginia, is five hundred miles.

It took Harriet three years to make her second quilt. We don't know how much money she earned for her labor. But she must have looked forward to the extra income, for hard times continued in the Powers family. In 1894 Armstead could not pay his taxes. Perhaps the money troubles were too much for him. Sometime around 1895 he left his wife of forty years and moved to another farm a few miles away.

Harriet had probably been earning her own income for some time. She felt independent enough to stay on the farm and to manage her affairs. She paid the yearly taxes, perhaps with money made from sewing. In 1897 she mortgaged one acre of land to buy a buggy for $16.89. And by 1898 she completed the second quilt for presentation to Reverend Hall.

Four years later in 1902, Atlanta University held a conference called "The Negro Artisan." Maybe it was this second lovely child of Harriet's imagination that inspired the board of trustees to sponsor the event. Like her first story quilt, the second was a song, a heavenly harmony of shape and color that we can listen to again and again.

## • 1898–1911 •

"My father was a full-blooded African. He was about eighteen years old when they brought him over. They just brought 'em on over to Georgy and sold 'em."

*CHANEY MACK*

Harriet made both of her story quilts with a sewing method called appliqué. *Appliqué* means "applied work." Instead of making her designs with patchwork or embroidery, she "applied," or stitched cloth to a background fabric.

Many cultures have used this process. Hand-appliquéd textiles were made by the Spanish in the 1100s and by the Italians in the fourteenth century. American Indians, West Africans, and Tibetan lamas, or holy men, have used the same method. Early in this century Eskimo women still painted

"Adam and Eve in the garden. Eve tempted by the serpent. Adam's rib by which Eve was made. The sun and moon. God's all-seeing eye and God's merciful hand." The hand, eye, sun, and moon in Harriet's picture are similar to the figures in the African story banner *(facing page)*.

strips of dried seal intestine and appliquéd them onto clothes for decoration.

Appliqué was quite popular with American women in Harriet's time. They decorated bags, hats, pincushions, tablecloths, curtains, and even stools with trees, leaves, stalks, and flowers. Needleworkers used pattern books to cut designs out of silk, satin, and velvet. Often they rimmed the cutout with braids, beads, or feathers. These were tacked down in large stitches of gold thread.

Harriet decided on appliqué for her quilts because she had seen it all her life. She knew this method was saved for the best quilts, the ones that showed off the needleworker's skills. But she did not choose to make the floral designs that were so common in her day. Nor did she follow the geometric forms used by the American Indian. Instead, she cut out figures, animals, sunbursts, stars,

The bird, the lion, and the cross in this banner appear in both of Harriet's quilts. In Benin, West Africa, the cross is a symbol for Lisa, the sun-god.

and crosses that appear to come from Africa.

How did Harriet learn to make these figures? She was an African American with African ancestors. She might have seen her mother, an aunt, or a grandfather making similar designs in the slave cabins when she was growing up. It's possible that she knew someone who had been born in Africa, then captured and brought directly to Georgia as a slave.

In the kingdom of Dahomey (now Benin) in West Africa, men have been "workers in cloth" and experts in appliqué for generations. Like Harriet, they cut out figures of lions, birds, elephants, and fish from both light and dark cloth. The men pass the designs down to their sons, who pass them on again to their own sons.

The cloth-workers make appliquéd costumes to wear in religious dances. Appliqué

Appliqué cloth-workers in Abomey, Dahomey. *National Museum of African Art. Photograph by Eliot Elisofon, 1971.*

is a sign of rank, so they decorate umbrellas, flags, caps, and bonnets to wear as status symbols. Like Harriet, they also use appliqué as a kind of writing: Appliquéd funeral cloths tell a picture-story about the dead person. And like Harriet, they make story banners to tell events from their history. Just as she chose bright fabrics, their favorite colors are red, black, white, and gold.

In Ghana, near Benin, the Akan people have made appliquéd flags for hundreds of years. Entire families become members of military associations, or companies, each with its own flag. The flags feature colorful animal and human figures, as well as the ancient religious symbols of the moon and the stars. These symbols show the presence of the Islam religion in Africa.

Harriet's quilts have the same perspective as do African banners and flags—all can be viewed from only one direction. They are similar in size—all are wider than they are long. And they seem to be alike in purpose.

Her quilts are too wide and short for a bed. She may have made the first story-quilt as a flag for a fraternal lodge. It's likely that she belonged to one of these African-American helping organizations, since they were often

Harriet repeats the story of Noah and the animals that survived the flood by going aboard the ark, two by two. Repetition is important in both African and African-American music, as seen in this religious song:

We'll run and never tire,
We'll run and never tire,
We'll run and never tire,
Jesus sets poor sinners free.

The fish in this African story banner look like Harriet's whale *(facing page)*.

connected to churches. And her second story-quilt looks more like a banner for a wall than a cover for a bed.

Harriet Powers's quilts are like crossroads where the best ideas of many cultures meet. She used the universal method of appliqué stitching. She cut out African animals to express biblical ideas. And she combined them all in an American quilt. Her creations remind us that men and women of every color, country, and religion are the same: We all want to decorate our lives with beautiful, useful art.

We know little about Harriet's final history. By 1900 only three of her children were still alive. One daughter, Lizzie, still lived at home. Marshall was a bricklayer, and Alonzo was a farmer and Baptist preacher. In 1901 Harriet and Armstead agreed to sell the remaining two acres of land that they had owned together. She continued to live in the Sandy Creek area for another nine years.

In 1910 the elderly Harriet moved a few miles south to Buck Branch, where most of the population was African American. Perhaps she was ill and needed to be with friends or relatives. From tax records it is clear that she lived in poverty. Everything she owned in 1911 was worth only seventy dollars. She died that year at the age of seventy-four.

There are one million African-American quilts in the United States. The oldest of these were made by unidentified slaves. Sometimes the only way to recognize a slave-made quilt is to look for African-American hair that might have fallen into the cotton batting sandwiched between the top and bottom of the quilt. Because the identity of so many slave quilters is unknown, we are lucky to have Harriet's full name. And since most slaves couldn't write, we are even luckier to have Jennie Smith's written record of Harriet's words. They help us know what stories she meant to tell.

"Jonah casted over board of the ship and swallowed by a whale. Turtles."

Harriet was born and raised on a plantation and lived the rest of her life on a small farm. She may never have seen a town bigger than Athens, Georgia, or left the state of her birth. But when she sat down each evening to work on a story quilt, she traveled to a different world.

In her celestial realm, slices of moon float in quilted heavens. Angels dance around calico stars, and birds fly through a cotton sky. Harriet Powers's quilts take us to that special spot inside the artist's mind where pictures are set free. By looking at her stories, we can make the trip as often as we wish.

# AFTERWORD

"Oh, watch that star, see how it run."

*Georgia slave shout song*

• • •

Jennie Smith got a bargain when she paid five dollars for Harriet's quilt. Although that would be seventy-five dollars in current money, quilts now cost hundreds, even thousands of dollars. But no amount, large or small, could buy Harriet's quilts today. Priceless treasures, they are stars in the world of African-American folk art.

When Jennie Smith died in 1946, she did not leave the quilt to any particular person. The man who settled her estate eventually gave it to the Smithsonian Institution, a collection of fourteen museums in Washington, D.C., that belongs to the people of the United States. Harriet's creation is in the National Museum of American History— the perfect place to see her quilted his-tory of African-American textiles, religion, and folklore.

Reverend Hall left Harriet's second story-quilt to his son. It was then sold to a folk art collector, Maxim Korolik. He donated his art collection, including the quilt, to the Museum of Fine Arts, Boston, in 1964.

Museums can protect the cloth and thread in antique textiles like Harriet's quilts. To prevent further fading and damage caused by light, air, and use, old needlework is stored in rooms with controlled temperatures. When quilts are displayed for public view, they are hung behind glass under dim lights.

Both of Harriet's "darling offspring," as Jennie Smith called Harriet's first story-quilt, are being carefully preserved for study and enjoyment. Now future generations can marvel at the charming shapes, learn from the stories, and admire the genius of Harriet Powers.

# SELECTED SOURCES

A few of the books and articles used to research this book:

Adams, Marie Jeanne. "The Harriet Powers Pictorial Quilts." *Afro-American Folk Art and Crafts*. Edited by William Ferris. Jackson: University Press of Mississippi, 1983.

Fry, Gladys-Marie. *Stitched from the Soul: Slave Quilts from the Ante-Bellum South*. New York: Dutton, 1990.

Herskovits, Melville J., and Frances S. Herskovits. "The Art of Dahomey: Brass-Casting and Appliqué Cloths." *American Magazine of Art*, February 1934, 67–76.

Killion, Ronald, and Charles Waller, eds. *When I Was Chillun Down on Marster's Plantation*. Savannah, Georgia: Beehive Press, 1973.

Vlach, John Michael. *The Afro-American Tradition in Decorative Arts*. Athens: University of Georgia Press, 1990.

# INDEX  Page numbers for illustrations/captions are in *italics*

Harriet decorated her apron with a cross, a sunburst, and a scalloped hem.
*Museum of Fine Arts, Boston, Massachusetts.*